# SESAME STREET

## MY ADVENTURES
### WITH
# ELMO
## AND FRIENDS

This book was especially written
Lexy Keslin
With love from
Grandma and Grandpa

By Kate Andresen
Copyright ©2007 Sesame Workshop
ISBN 1 875676 24 4

# Rise and Shine on Sesame Street!

Rise and shine! The sun is coming up!

It was a beautiful day, with blue skies and fluffy white clouds.

On Sesame Street, little monsters and birds and grouches were out and about, enjoying the early morning sunshine.

Lexy lived not far from Sesame Street at 235 Sycamore Lane in Munster. Elmo and Lexy were having a sleepover at Elmo's house.

"Rise and shine, Elmo!" called Lexy softly.

"Let's go outside and play!" said Elmo as he jumped out of bed.

"Sure Elmo! I would love to go outside to play with you! Then, we can go to Hooper's Store for breakfast. Sydney, Delaney and Paige will be there, too," Lexy replied.

"Maybe our other friends will come with us, too," Elmo said.

It was a glorious day on Sesame Street! In the street outside Elmo's house, the garbage collectors were emptying the garbage cans.

This was Oscar's favorite time of the day! He wakes up early to watch the garbage collectors and he loves to join in by banging on the cans as they are carried by.

"Bang those cans!" yelled Oscar. "That's it boys! Crash 'em! Clank 'em! Heh-heh-heh."

"Will Oscar come out to play with Elmo and Lexy?" asked Elmo.

"Nah! I'm busy, and it's too nice out! Now SCRAM!" replied Oscar.

Further down the street they saw the Count. He was up early, too, delivering newspapers.

"Rise and shine, everyone! It's a wonderful day for counting! One newspaper! Two newspapers! Three newspapers!"

As Elmo and Lexy walked passed Bert and Ernie's house, they heard a trumpet playing.

Elmo called through their open bedroom window, "Ernie, Bert! Want to come to play with Elmo and Lexy?" Ernie was trying to wake up his buddy, Bert, who was still trying to sleep.

"Hi, Elmo! Hi, Lexy! Sorry, we can't come out just now," Ernie said. "Bert is still sleeping."

"OK," said Elmo. But he was disappointed.

"Don't worry, Elmo. We'll still have fun—just the two of us," Lexy said.

When they got to Big Bird's house, they heard singing and splashing.

"La! La! La! La! La!" Big Bird sang as he splashed in his morning bath with some friends.

"Hey, Big Bird! Want to come outside and play?" asked Elmo.

"Gee, I'd love to Elmo, but I promised I'd help my friend Henry to look after his baby brother," replied Big Bird.

"Oh, OK. Have fun, Big Bird," called Elmo.

As Elmo and Lexy turned the corner they saw Herry Monster running towards them.

"Herry Monster!" called Elmo. "Want to come and play with Elmo and Lexy?"

"Must finish my run, but I'll see you at Hooper's for breakfast," replied Herry Monster, huffing and puffing as he jogged passed them.

"Come on, Elmo. I'll race you to the park," said Lexy.

But when they passed by the bakery, they stopped. In the window there were yummy cookies and cakes and the smell of freshly baked bread wafted out through the door.

"Hmmmm… Elmo is hungry now. Elmo thinks it is time for breakfast," he said breathing deeply.

Lexy agreed. "OK, Elmo. Let's go for breakfast now."

When they got to Hooper's Store it was already filled with happy monsters and grouches. There was Benny the bellhop and Baby Natasha and her Mommy and Daddy. Herry Monster was there too.

"Hey Elmo! Hey Lexy!" called Herry Monster cheerfully. "Come and join us!"

Elmo and Lexy were very happy to see all their friends. After breakfast they all went outside to play. After all, it was a beautiful day on Sesame Street and all the monsters and birds and grouches had come out to play!

# Elmo's Talent Show

Elmo loves music! One day he decided to hold a talent show. The theme would be FEELINGS. Elmo invited all the Sesame Street gang to perform. As the show was about to start, Elmo peeped from behind the curtain and announced...

*"Oh welcome, oh welcome to our little play.*
*We are ever so glad you could join us today!*
*We are going to sing about FEELINGS! And so,*
*Please open the curtain and on with the show!"*

Elmo asked Lexy to be his special helper. Her job was to organize the performers and open and close the curtains. Sydney, Delaney and Paige were also back stage. They were helping the Sesame Street gang get ready for their performances.

At last, Lexy opened the curtain and Elmo and Herry Monster danced on to center stage and sang...

*"We are two furry monsters, one red and one blue.*
*We can count up to twenty and tie our own shoes.*
*We can sing oh-so-sweetly—*
*OR SHOUT VERY LOUD!*
*Have you guessed how we feel?*
*We're both feeling PROUD!"*

Next, it was Mumford the Magician's turn to weave his magic.

*"Mumford's my name, many tricks I perform.*
*I pull rabbits from hats. I can make a rainstorm!*
*A-LA-PEANUT-BUTTER SANDWICHES!"*

He waved his magic wand and suddenly there were five large, fluffy white rabbits hopping around on the stage.

*"Good heavens, my rabbits are extra-large-sized!*
*It's snowing, not raining—even I feel SURPRISED!"*

Lexy quickly closed the curtains. Sydney, Delaney and Paige caught the rabbits before they could escape! Grover, Bert, Ernie and their friends were next to perform and they began their song.

*"Pizza and ice cream, my little pet fish,*
*my warm fuzzy blankie, my favorite dish,*
*cute furry kitties, and honey on toast—*
*these things are all nice, but I LOVE MOMMY most!"*

The curtain closed and it was time for intermission.

Cookie Monster had baked some cookies and he invited everyone on stage to join him. In a very loud voice, he announced…

*"Here's a big plate of cookies all gooey and sweet— with big chocolate chips! It's time for us to eat!"*

*"When me have some cookies,*
*that make me feel GLAD!*
*But when the plate's empty…*
(Hmm. Maybe just one or two to see how they
taste. Mmmm! Delicious! Gobble, gobble!)
*me feel very SAD!"*

Cookie Monster ate
most of the cookies!

It was time for the show to begin again and Lexy opened the curtains once more. Oscar was at center stage and he was beating a very loud tune on his drum.

Bert and Ernie also came on and performed amazing tricks with their kite and ball. Bert spun the ball on his finger and bounced it between his legs while Ernie's kite danced and weaved gracefully above the audience.

Big Bird sat to one side of the stage and began telling the story...

*"When Oscar's up late and makes too much noise, when people at play group will not share their toys, when my birdseed pancakes turn out to be lumpy, I sit in a corner and feel really GRUMPY!"*

"But now, I am HAPPY to call on Bert to dance for you," announced Big Bird.

Bert was dressed in baggy brown pants with suspenders. He sang as he danced across the stage…

*"To show you my feeling, I'll do a short dance. Now I feel EMBARRASSED in polka-dot pants!"* Bert exclaimed as he ran off the stage.

Poor Bert! Lexy closed the curtains.

Soon, Elmo's show drew to a close and he called
on all his friends to gather on stage for a final
song.

*"When we're feeling HAPPY, we stand on our heads
and we dance all around and we jump on our beds!
We sing tra-la-la and we laugh ho-ho-ho!
When we're feeling HAPPY, we let the world know!"*

Then Elmo made a special announcement.

"Elmo hopes you have enjoyed Elmo's show. Elmo would like to thank everyone for helping and performing. Elmo would especially like to thank his friend, Lexy, who is celebrating her birthday today," he announced. "Yes, it is February 18th, Lexy's special day!"

Prairie Dawn sat down at the piano and everyone started singing...

*"Happy birthday to you, Happy birthday to you Happy birthday, dear Lexy, Happy birthday to you! Hip, hip, hooray!"*

What a great way to spend her birthday— surrounded by the Sesame Street gang and Sydney, Delaney and Paige.

# Sleep Tight Sesame Street

Elmo was playing a game of monster tag with his friends in the park late one afternoon. They were having lots of fun! All too soon the sun started going down and it was time to go home. It was almost bedtime for little monsters.

On his way home, Elmo saw his friend Lexy outside her house at 235 Sycamore Lane in Munster. Lexy was talking to Little Bird who was getting ready for bed. Splish, splash! Little Bird shook his feathers in his warm bath.

"Hi, Lexy, want to come sleepover at Elmo's?" asked Elmo.

"That will be fun! Wait while I ask my mommy," replied Lexy. Soon, Lexy came out carrying her overnight bag.

"Goodnight, Little Bird," called Lexy.

"Sleep tight, Little Bird," said Elmo.

As they continued on their way to Elmo's house,
they walked by Herry Monster and Flossie's house.
Flossie wasn't sleepy yet so Herry and Flossie did
toe touches.

"...Seven! Eight! Nine! Ten!" panted Herry
Monster. "Are you getting sleepy, Flossie?" She
shook her head.

"Good night, Herry," waved Elmo.

"Sleep tight, Elmo," called Flossie.

A little further on Elmo and Lexy came across Oscar. He was reading his book, *Mother Grouch Rhymes.*

*"Little Boy Grouch, come blow your kazoo.*
*Take a mud bath and eat anchovy stew…"*

He closed his book. It was getting too dark to read now and Oscar was a sleepy grouch.

"Sleep tight, Oscar," called Elmo and Lexy.

"Yucchy dreams," said Oscar as he settled into his garbage can for the night.

"Oh, look! Big Bird is already tucked up in bed with Radar, his teddy bear. Hope Big Bird has a good night," said Elmo.

"Thank you, Elmo," replied Big Bird. "I must do one last thing before I go to sleep." Then Big Bird started singing a lullaby.

*"Rock-a-bye, Radar, snug in my nest.*
*Time for us both to lie down and rest!*
*Sleep tight, little bear,"* sang Big Bird.

"Hey, Elmo. Hey, Lexy," called Ernie from his window as he, too, was preparing for bed.

In Ernie's window box, sleepy Twiddlebugs snuggled under their leaf blankets.

"Lexy is coming to Elmo's house for a sleepover," said Elmo.

"That's nice," replied Ernie. "Have a good time."

"Good night, Ernie. Sleep tight, little Twiddlebugs," said Elmo.

Everything was quiet on Sesame Street. Monsters and birds and grouches and Twiddlebugs slept soundly in their beds.

By now, Elmo and Lexy were also tucked up safely in their beds.

"Good night, Elmo. Thank you for inviting me to your house," said Lexy.

"Sleep tight, Lexy. Sweet dreams. Tomorrow Elmo and Lexy will go to the park again and play with all our friends," replied Elmo sleepily.

   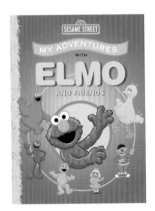

For our entire selection of books, please visit www.identitydirect.com

This personalized Sesame Street Elmo and Friends book was especially created for Lexy Keslin of 235 Sycamore Lane, Munster with love from Grandma and Grandpa.

Additional books ordered may be mailed separately — please allow a few days for differences in delivery times.

If you would like to receive additional My Adventure Book forms, please contact:

**My Adventure Books**

inquiry@identitydirect.com
www.identitydirect.com